GINNY

A RAM
FOR ISAAC

JOURNEYFORTH
Greenville, South Carolina

Library of Congress Cataloging-in Publication Data

Merritt, Ginny, 1947
   A ram for Isaac / Ginny Merritt.
      p. cm.
   Summary: In biblical times, young Isaac and his friends have a good time accompanying Abraham to Mt. Moriah, but when father and son climb the mountain alone, Isaac learns the depth of Abraham's trust in God even as they both are tested.
   ISBN 978-1-59166-983-8 (saddlestitch : alk. paper)
  1. Abraham (Biblical patriarch)—Juvenile fiction. 2. Isaac (Biblical patriarch)—Juvenile fiction. [1. Abraham (Biblical patriarch)—Fiction. 2. Isaac (Biblical patriarch)—Fiction. 3. Trust in God—Fiction. 4. Bible. O.T.—History of Biblical events—Fiction. 5. Fathers and sons—Fiction.] I. Title.
   PZ7.M545443Ram 2009
   [E]—dc22

2008055116

Design by Rita Golden
Illustrations by Keith Neely
© 2009 by BJU Press
Greenville, SC 29614
JourneyForth Books is a division of BJU Press

**Dedicated with lots of love
to my own Bible students:
first my children, Ann Elyse and Hans,
and now my grandsons, Odin and Cyrus.**

There is a Lamb for us.

This story is my idea of what might have happened
in the account recorded in Genesis 22:1–14.
The Scripture does not give Isaac a specific age
but calls him a lad or a youth.
I have chosen to think of him as about twelve years old.
Please read the Scripture first
and let God show you
what He wants you to learn from the story.

—g.m.

CONTENTS

CHAPTER 1...........1
CHAPTER 2.........5
CHAPTER 3..........8
CHAPTER 4.........15
CHAPTER 5.........21

CHAPTER 1

"Catch, Kemuel! Catch!" I yelled. I threw a dried gourd to him. Kemuel was one of my best friends.

He and I had another good friend named Dedan. The three of us started on an adventure one morning with my father.

We three boys rolled rocks and looked for lizards. We ran after rabbits as the morning sun rose. Then we raced back to Father. He laughed at me and my friends.

It is not unusual for Father to laugh at me. My name means "laughter." My name is Isaac.

My parents say they laughed when God told them I would be born. They were old when God told them that. They were too old to have a child! But they say nothing is impossible for our God, Jehovah. Still, they laughed and named me Isaac. They say they have been laughing with delight ever since.

I am always eager for adventure. Most days I stay in the camp with my mother. She taught me to tend the fire. She lets me look for wild vegetables and herbs with her. She and Father gave me my own pet goat. I named her Shinah. I like to take care of her. When my work with Mother is done, I play with my friends.

I love my mother. I like being with her and the others in the camp. But I like it even better when I work with Father. He takes me with him to check on the herds and the men who work for him. It makes me feel grown-up and important.

One day a surprise came. Early one morning, my father whispered to me outside the tent. "Son, today we will not go to check on the well in the stony eastern field as we had planned. Instead we will go on an adventure."

"You and your friends Kemuel and Dedan and I will take a journey with our donkey. We will go to Mt. Moriah. We will make an offering to Jehovah there. Hurry and get your things. Be quiet and do not awaken your mother."

I slipped away to get Kemuel and Dedan. The day was still a quiet grey. We whispered while we packed up. When we left, we passed my mother's tent. My heart beat hard with excitement. I was sure she would hear it and wake up.

Mother's maid was already stirring the fire for breakfast. Father talked with her in the chilly morning air. He told her to remind Mother that we would return in a few days, just as he had told her.

She said, "Yes, Master Abraham."

That is my father's name—Abraham. It means "Father of Many Nations." That makes *me* laugh, because I'm his and Mother's only son!

Then we all moved quietly away from the tent village: Kemuel, Dedan, Father, the donkey, and I.

CHAPTER 2

The sun rose in front of us. It cast long shadows of the rocks and brush that lined our way. My friends and I played and ran and returned to Father. He laughed and swung the water skin to us when we got thirsty. Mostly he rode silently on our donkey.

We slept under the stars for two nights. It was different from being at home. There we could hear the women chattering as they made meals. We could hear the men talking as they told of their trials with Father's flocks.

Out here it was quiet. Father let us boys help with
the fire and the cooking. When our stomachs were
full and the embers burned bright, he told us stories.
He told us of a land far away in the East where there
were many people and houses and shops. He told us
of my grandfather Terah and his grandson Lot and
of their long journey on camels away from that land.

I asked Father if he had been frightened to go to a country he had never seen. He told me he was frightened sometimes. But he learned to trust in Jehovah. When Jehovah said to obey, His help would come with our obedience. I wasn't quite sure what that meant. But I liked listening to him.

During the day, Father kept his eyes on the horizon where the land meets the sky. We were headed to a mountain we could see a long way ahead. Mt. Moriah. The mountain range looked like a giant tent village jutting up into the blue sky.

On the third morning, Father told Kemuel and Dedan to stay by our camp and keep the fire burning. He told them we would return by evening. He asked them to have a meal ready for the four of us. He said that they should not fool around or let the donkey run away.

Their eyes grew big, and they dropped the stones they were holding. I think they were scared. They had not been left alone before to take care of things.

Then we went on, Father and I.

CHAPTER 3

On that third day Father and I began to climb the great mountain, Moriah. I was so excited. He let me carry the heavy pack of wood for the worship fire. He told me I was growing big and strong. He said that soon I would begin to learn how to handle his flocks and fields with him. Then he sighed deeply.

Perhaps he was thinking he might die sometime and I would have to carry on in his place. Father was very old. I did not like to think of life without him. I sighed, too, and looked again at Father. He had coals from the campfire in one hand and the big knife for butchering our sheep in the other. I was big enough to carry the wood, but not grown-up enough yet to handle those tools.

Suddenly I exclaimed, "Father! You have forgotten something!"

Father stopped just above me to catch his breath on the steep slope. He turned and looked at me patiently.

"What is it, Isaac?"

"We have wood and fire and a knife, but we have no sacrifice!"

As old as he was, my father's mind was a fine one. He never forgot a single thing about his business. How could he forget something as important as an animal for our sacrifice?

"Isaac, what you say is true. You are an observant boy. But God said that He will provide the lamb. I do not understand how He will do this, but I am trusting Him. You must learn to do that also, my son."

He went on gently, but firmly, "When Jehovah speaks, do not doubt Him. Only obey. He will give you strength and supplies. Listen carefully to what He says, and do only that. Do it quickly. If you wait, your fears and questions may bar your ability to hear Him again. Keep your eyes ahead. Do not look at the thousand things around you that will keep you from obedience. Do you understand?"

I wasn't sure I did, but I said, "Yes, Father, I . . . I think so."

"And, Isaac, my son, today I want to ask you one thing. Please trust me as I do what Jehovah has told me to do. It will help you to learn to trust Him as well. Can you do that for me, Isaac?"

Father's brown eyes burned into mine. He frightened me. Never before had he talked this way to me. The wrinkles around his eyes reminded me of how wise he was. The shine in his eyes assured me of his love for me.

He and Mother always told me of how much laughter I had brought into their lives. If only we could laugh now and break this awful stillness.

I looked back at him. I wanted to run down the mountain to my friends and throw rocks with them. I wanted to run the two-day journey back to Mother and feel her soft arms around me.

But Father watched and waited.

My eyes blinked back . . . what was it? Sand? Was there sand in my eyes? No, there were tears. My hand brushed away the wetness, and I breathed deeply. Father touched my shoulder.

Again he spoke.
"Isaac. Will you trust me?"

He smiled, and I shifted the weight of the pack on my back.
"Yes, Father. I will trust you."

CHAPTER 4

Father had asked me to trust him as he obeyed Jehovah.
I told him I would, but my mind churned with questions.
The top of the mountain now seemed to burn in the light of
the midmorning sun. We went on. Father's sandals picked
their way among the stones ahead of us.

At the top of the mountain, we took a drink from the
water skin and rested briefly. Far below I could see the
clearing where Kemuel and Dedan and our good donkey
stirred around the campfire. Smoke rose up the mountainside.
I wondered what my friends were thinking and doing. So
much had changed since we left them.

Father began to get ready for our worship. I helped him unload the wood from my pack. My eyes wandered around the rocks and brush near us. I saw a dove dart away, but I saw nothing else that we could use for the sacrifice.

The wood was ready. We were both sweating in the sun. The air was still. I heard only our breathing and our feet shuffling in the sand.

Surely now Father would say something.

Instead he did a strange thing. He began to bind me with ropes. Each time he touched me, it was with love. Each time our eyes met, his said, *Trust me*.

My heart was jumping like a little goat. He picked me up and laid me on the stone altar we had made together.

My mind raced. *What is Father doing? Is he going to kill me? Am **I** the sacrifice? No. **NO!***

I wanted to run away. The ropes were hurting me. I was so hot . . . and so cold . . . and so frightened. But Father had said . . . he had just said, "Trust me."

And I had promised.

He raised his knife. The sun shone off the bright blade. I could not see for a moment.

Everything was quiet.

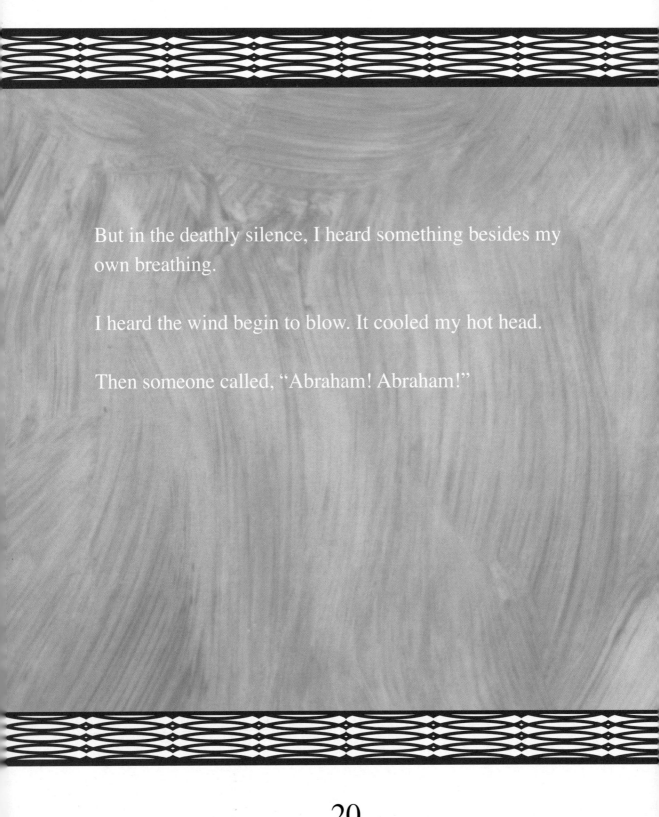

But in the deathly silence, I heard something besides my own breathing.

I heard the wind begin to blow. It cooled my hot head.

Then someone called, "Abraham! Abraham!"

CHAPTER 5

Father called, "Here I am!"

I twisted my head around to look. The voice that had just
called his name told him not to harm me. Father lowered his
arm. He, too, looked around. We saw no one.

He loosened my ropes. I jumped down beside him, my thin
legs shaking. I felt the softness of his robe against my cold arm.

Then we heard a noise again. The wind was still blowing, and there, in the lifted leaves of the thicket, was a ram, a fat ram, a fine white ram.

It was like one of Father's own best stock. Its big horns were tangled in the branches. It was struggling to get away, kicking sand and rocks. It looked like it might tear the bush out by its roots.

"Father, where did the white ram come from? I saw nothing before."

"Did I not tell you, my son?" Father's warm eyes burst with laughter. "If you obey Jehovah, He will give you strength and supplies. Has He not done this?"

He took the ram with no trouble. Together we sacrificed on that mountain. I had never had such cause to worship my father's God. Life had been given in place of mine.

We sang the songs and prayed the prayers I had been taught since I was a small child. But never had I sung and prayed them so! My heart was full. I felt a head taller as I stood beside Father. We watched the smoke curl upward. The smell of the roasting ram filled my nostrils.

Truly God had provided. Father was right. I had seen His supply with my own eyes.

Before we left the mountaintop, Father said we would name this holy place. "Jehovahjireh," he said and smiled at me.

I smiled back and agreed, " 'The Lord will provide.' The Lord *has* provided!"

Together we walked back down the mountain. Father's steps seemed lighter, as if he had become younger. My steps felt firmer, as if I had grown older.

"How glad Mother will be to see us!" I said.

We looked at each other, and we laughed.